I dedicate this book to my wife.

Minamahal Kita

ACKNOWLEDGEMENTS

I would like to thank my wife Valarie and my children Amoreena, Dom, Mark, Brooke and Hannah for believing that Ants can Surf! Thank you for understanding me and truly loving me. God has given me the best gift ever...my family.

Thanks also to my mom and dad for all their love and sacrifices. You have always been there for me. Thanks to my brothers Ada Rich, George and Bob. I am also so grateful for my wonderful nieces and nephews for listening to all my stories.

Special thanks go to my good friend and the best Webmaster in the world, Cris Simac. Your dedication and patience have brought our surfing ants to surf the World Wide Web.

I am truly grateful to my friend and mentor John "Mr. Snap On Man" Collier who gave me the strength to believe in myself.

Thank you Lonni for bringing my vision and dream to life. Our characters are alive and will be forever.

I want to give big thanks to Pat Hinz for her artistic talent in creating the AOR rice bowls and for her kind spirit.

Thank you to my editor Carrie Yamato for taking the time to sort through all my thoughts on paper.

Thanks to Diane Vircic, the best network person alive.

Special thanks to all my buddies at Ralph's Grocery company: Scott Sudoko, Ralph Nash, Donna Collver, Sandy Bilan, Rosalie Carswell and Mary Flanagan, and of course local boy Ted Wada. You are all part of the AOR Team!

Thank you also to:

Christina Ferrelli for all her help for getting the word out in the Ralph's newsletters.

Alex Mecl, my business consultant. You gave me direction and helped me stay focused.

My friends in Long Beach - Eddie Moretti and long-time friend Ron Reed.

I cannot forget to thank the Schooner crew: Ty and Susan McCoy, Carrol Roberts and my buddie "Happy Jane."

Mac for her efforts early in the project.

Will Olstad and Chromatic Litho.

Rusty Granados for his expertise.

Ants on the Rainbow...
You'll Never Know

By James Daos

Art By Lonni

Hi! My name is Lil' Hannah. As you can see, I look like a tiny creature known as an ant. But, I am far from an ordinary ant. My family and I are very unique. We belong to a colony of ants that surf. That's right! I said surf! We are some radical surfing ants!

I know, you're probably thinking, "Don't ants get antsy around water?" Yes, most ants do. But that's what makes it so unreal. We enjoy water and we love to surf!

My family and I live on a tiny island in the South Pacific Ocean. The island has beautiful tropical rain forests along with a few barren spots. Of course, the island is surrounded by waves! I love it!

We live in one of the shells that are scattered along a creek that runs down to the blue sea.

The Fire Ants claim a barren area on the other side of the island. Their leader, Fink, and the rest of the Fire Ants live in the stump of an old tree that was hit by lightning years ago. The Fire Ants are dangerous and like to hurt other creatures. These guys are nuts!

The evil Enslaver Ants live in a treeless, rocky area of the island. A powerful ant named Smasher bosses them around all day long. Smasher and his gang live in dark tunnels which were dug by his soldier ants.

Digging tunnels is hard work, so Smasher and his gang are always trying to force other ants to do the digging for them.

When the weather is fierce and thunder booms across the sky, Smasher and his soldier ants come out of the tunnels and raid other colonies.

The colonies on our side of the island try to stay far away from them.

My Grandpa George had a blue stone necklace that was handed down to him from his Grandfather. Ant legend says the necklace has magical powers, which will guide the colony to a place called paradise.

Everyone knew Smasher wanted the blue stone necklace, and that he would do anything to get it.

When he was a young ant, Grandpa George was a mighty warrior. A long time ago during a terrible storm, Smasher raided Grandpa George's colony and tried to steal the blue stone necklace. Smasher lost his eye in that battle. That's why he wears a black patch over his right eye. Smasher makes his soldier ants wear a patch so he isn't the only one who looks different.

My father, Jimmy D, guarded the necklace after my Grandpa George. Now, I am the one who wears and protects it.

My Grandma Kane is a soft-spoken lady with a big heart. She walks with a slight limp so to help keep her balance, Grandpa George made her a walking stick out of sugar cane. She is so sweet. That's why we call her Grandma Kane.

She also has a kind and gentle spirit.

She spends a lot of time cooking. Her specialty is a killer fried-rice dish.

My mom, Nessa, was raised in a colony that lived in a beautiful old piece of driftwood along a peaceful riverbank. They are a colony of craft ants. Mom's special talent is making umbrellas out of bamboo cane and banana leaves. These umbrellas would keep the colony dry when the tropical showers arrived. Pretty clever, huh?

Her family also has a treasure, "The Book of Ant Wisdom." This book contains many wise sayings and also gives directions on how to survive on the island. Mom is the protector of the book for her colony.

My mom and dad came from two rare ant colonies but share something in common. They both had to guard their lives and their treasure from Smasher, Fink and their gangs.

I come from a big family. I have four older brothers and sisters. Ambella, my oldest sister, is very artistic. She knows how to make umbrellas from bamboo cane and banana leaves just like my mom... well almost like my mom.

She surfs with a lot of grace and style. She likes to walk the board and Hang Five from the nose of her board. This is a really cool surf move.

Ambella can always be counted on to do the right thing. When mom and dad aren't around, she's in charge. She spends a lot of time reading from "The Book of Ant Wisdom." Some nights, mom lets her read to us.

Matu is the next oldest of my brothers and sisters. He is amazingly strong and brave. That's because he is always working out by paddling his board in the ocean and climbing up and down hills.

Matu likes to fish and forage. He collects twine, twigs and rocks and can make the most amazing things out of them.

Matu is a power surfer, which means he uses his strength to ride the waves. He can switch his stance on his surfboard.

Matu is happy to take on part of the duties of guarding the colony. Smasher and Fink better watch out. Matu has some surprises in store for them!

DC may be younger than Matu but he stands a few inches taller than Matu. DC stands for Double Curl. When my dad took him to the ocean for the first time, DC pointed at the waves and his first words were "double curl," so my dad named him DC for short.

He likes to tell jokes, pull pranks and show off. His love of showing off has helped him master just about every surf move. He can even pull off an occasional aerial. It's hard not to laugh when you're with DC.

Brookey is just a few years older than me. She loves to dye cloth and sew her own clothes. She collects seashells and makes really cool surf jewelry. Brookey is a courageous surfer girl and will paddle out in any conditions. Her two favorite moves are a radical cutback and an outrageous off the lip. Brookey loves to try anything her brothers can do (in and out of the water).

Peakie is Brookey's friend. Compared to other parrots Peakie is very tiny. Once, during a terrible storm, the wind swept Peakie up and over the island's highest mountain and right into Brookey's arms. They have been best buddies ever since.

Then there's me, Lil' Hannah. I love playing musical instruments. My favorite is the guitar, but I never go anywhere without my flute. My family says I rock!

I also love to go fishing with my brothers and making different crafts with my sisters.

I may be the baby but I can surf with my brothers and sisters without any problem. I can even do a 360 on a wave, front side and back side!

I don't go anywhere without the blue stone necklace since it became my job to guard it. My dad told me all about its history and how it may lead us to paradise someday. I guard it with all my heart!

I like it when Dad tells us stories. One of my favorites is how he and my mom met. You wont believe it, but they met because of Smasher and a wild storm.

My dad's name is Jimmy D. When he was teenage ant, it was his job to guard the blue stone necklace. One day while the rest of the colony was out working, Jimmy D got bored and decided to go outside and play a game with some sticks and rocks. While he was playing, a big raindrop fell right smack on his head. Jimmy D looked up and saw the beautiful day was turning dark and stormy. Suddenly thunder split the air sending Jimmy D running home. It was definitely a scary moment for him.

Jimmy D knew exactly what he was supposed to do. He put on the blue stone necklace and grabbed one of Grandma Kane's walking sticks and ran out the door in search of his colony. But gigantic shadows with spears were appearing out of the forest trail. It was Smasher's soldier ants! They were coming to raid! Jimmy D turned and ran as fast has he could towards the river. But the rain had made the path slippery and Jimmy D fell in the raging river.

The cane helped him keep his head barely above the water, but the current was so strong that it yanked the cane out of his arms.

Jimmy D remembered everything that his father had taught him. He grabbed the closest thing that floated by — a piece of bark with one twig and a leaf barely attached. And with all his might, he climbed on top of it.

Before he knew it, he was riding on top the river waves! He realized that by leaning left or right, he could control the direction of the bark. He had never felt such a rush of energy. He was stoked!

Something happened in that very moment which made him feel this was the beginning of something totally awesome.

Moving fast down the river on his bark board, he spotted another ant clinging to a twig struggling to keep her head above the raging river. He pulled her onto the bark board and they rode tandem down the river. As the storm began to pass, the river's current calmed down. They were able to get on the river's bank, where the beautiful Nessa, introduced herself, marveled at the bark board and told Jimmy D, how thankful she was that he saved her life. Isn't that so romantic?

They agreed that together they would try to find the trail back to their colonies.

Eventually, Nessa and Jimmy D made it back to Jimmy D's home. They discovered that what the storm didn't destroy, Smasher and his soldier ants did. It was a disaster.

Jimmy D did his best digging through the debris but all he could find was his red knapsack and one of the soldier ant's eye patches. He folded up the patch and put it in the sack. There was no sign of Grandpa George, Grandma Kane or anyone from his colony.

They moved through the storm-torn forest until they reached Nessa's home. The beautiful driftwood log, where her family lived, was destroyed. The small river, which ran beside her home, swept the entire colony into the water. They dug through the rubble. When she found a picnic basket, she opened it up and tears began streaming down her face.

"What's wrong?" asked Jimmy D? "I can't believe it! It's totally here" she told Jimmy D. "The Book of Ant Wisdom. It survived the storm. It's a miracle!"

After Nessa told Jimmy D about the books history and secrets, he shared the secrets of his blue stone necklace with her.

Nessa then read a page from the book:

Follow the path
through the trees,
over the rocks
to the sea,
wait for a sign,
and you'll know,
gather your family,
it's time to go.

Nessa and Jimmy D followed the book's directions. They made their way back to the river knowing it would eventually lead them to the sea.

Jimmy D found his bark board right where they had left it. While he searched for another one for Nessa, she drew these outrageous patterns on his board from the juice of a tropical plant.

"Cool! Those designs are tight!" exclaimed Jimmy D when he saw Nessa's artwork.

"What are you going to call these bark boards?" Nessa asked.

Jimmy D paused briefly and looked up at the sky to see if the storm had passed. He noticed some swirling clouds that resembled the ocean's surf and answered, "Surfboards. I am going to call them surfboards."

Pleased with the new name, they took their surfboards and paddled back into the river.

By board and by foot, they traveled what seemed like a thousand miles. Food was scarce where the storm hit hardest. But the further they traveled, the more food they found. It seemed too good to be true.

As they continued on their path, animals called out greetings. Birds sang from the trees. Insects scurried everywhere.

Jimmy D stopped to part a few giant leaves in their path and together they saw the most amazing thing — a waterfall glistening in the sun surrounded by fruit-filled trees and tropical flowers dropping petals into a crystal-clear pond below.

"Could this be ant paradise?" asked Jimmy D, as he took in the gorgeous colors of ripe fruit and wild flowers.

Nessa could only answer, "This takes my breath away."

As she began gathering fruit, Jimmy D grabbed his surfboard and stood on a flat rock. "Look, I'm in a tube of water," he yelled as the water from the cliffs above surrounded him.

Nessa watched Jimmy D ride his surfboard down the waterfall to the pond below. All she could do was smile and giggle. It was so good to hear laughter again. Nessa grabbed her board and joined him. It was a fun session.

As they splashed in the calm waters of the pond, two bubbly eyes rose to the surface. It was a tiny green frog.

"What are you silly ants doing in the water?" he asked.

"We're having fun and getting tubed," said Jimmy D.

"If it's tubes of water you want, follow the path behind the trees," said the frog. "It will lead you to the tide pools along the ocean's edge."

And with that, the tiny frog sank slowly into the pond.

They couldn't believe what they heard — the ocean! That meant they were close. They gathered their surfboards, picnic basket and knapsack and made their way along the last part of their long journey.

Jimmy D soon heard the sound of the waves. Nessa smelled the salty sea air. And before they knew it, they were at the beach. What an amazing sight!

They came across some seashells that were above the reach of the tides. This, they said, would be their home.

A dragonfly saw the happy couple and called out a greeting. "What's up?" he asked.

An old hermit crab came up on the rocks to see what all the noise was about. "Shh, I am trying to rest," he whispered.

A local group of ladybugs insisted on throwing them a party. "Hurray!" "Hurray!" they all chanted.

Under a pink sunset, and with their new friends as witnesses, Nessa and Jimmy D vowed to stay together and begin a new colony.

They dreamed someday they would find their families and the legendary paradise. But in the meantime, this was paradise.

Well, that's how it all began. That's how my mom and dad met, and how we all became surfing ants. My dad, Jimmy D and I have many more surf stories to tell as long as we can stay clear of Smasher, Fink and their gangs, so we will see you when the tide drops.

Oh yeah, one more thing, a wise ant once said "To surf or not to surf? There is no question!"

Look for more adventures of Ants on the Rainbow...You'll Never Know.

Surf Tip #1: Eat a banana before you surf. It will give you added energy.

Surf Glossary

Aerial — An outrageous surf maneuver that involves taking off from the lip of the wave, catching some distance in the air then landing back on the face of the wave.

Cut Back — Making a turn on the face of the wave that takes you back toward the white water.

Face — The unbroken surface of a wave, it is known as green water.

Grom — Short for Grommet, refers to any young or child surfer.

Hang Five — Riding with all five toes from one foot over the nose of the board. It's a very stylish move but one of the hardest for a long boarder.

Off The Lip — Turning the surfboard on the crest of the wave.

Switch Stance — When a surfer can surf with either his right or left foot forward on the board.

Tubed — Riding the hollow part of the wave. It is also known as getting barreled.

Three-Sixty (360°) — Spinning the board through 360 degrees on the face of the wave.

White Water — After the wave breaks, it forms white foam. This part of the wave can be very powerful. It is also known as white wash.